I0762336

# The Seventh Ogre

*Adapted and Illustrated by*

**LEE BROWN COYE**

**Afterword by Luis Ortiz**

LEE BROWN COYE - 1932 -

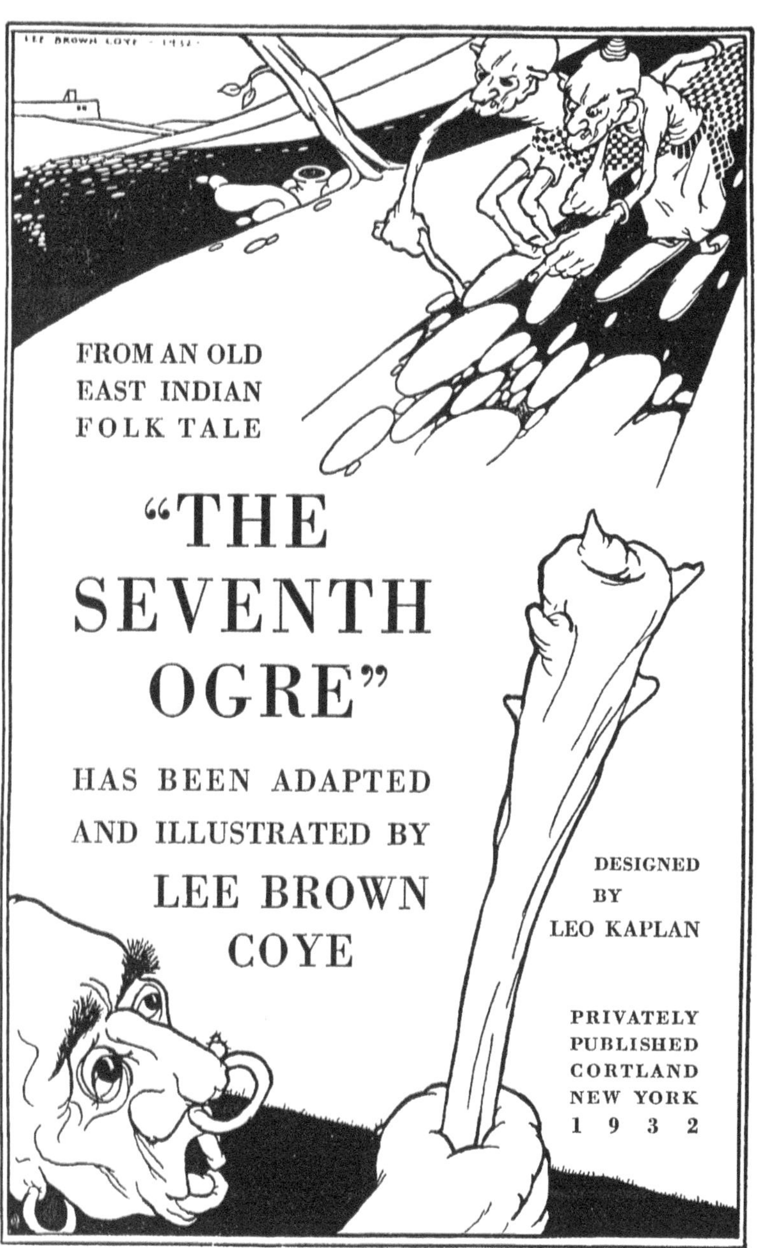
FROM AN OLD
EAST INDIAN
FOLK TALE
"THE
SEVENTH
OGRE"
HAS BEEN ADAPTED
AND ILLUSTRATED BY
LEE BROWN
COYE
DESIGNED
BY
LEO KAPLAN
PRIVATELY
PUBLISHED
CORTLAND
NEW YORK
1 9 3 2

# The Seventh Ogre

*Adapted and Illustrated by*
LEE BROWN COYE

*A Nonstop Press Facsimile Edition*

First Published 1932


Paperback ISBN 978-1-93-306564-9
Hardcover ISBN 978-1-933065-65-6



PRINTED IN THE UNITED STATES OF AMERICA
TYPESET IN BODONI

114 John Street, #981, New York, NY, 10272

www.nonstoppress.com

*To* Ruth

THE SEVENTH OGRE . . .

# THE SEVENTH OGRE . . .

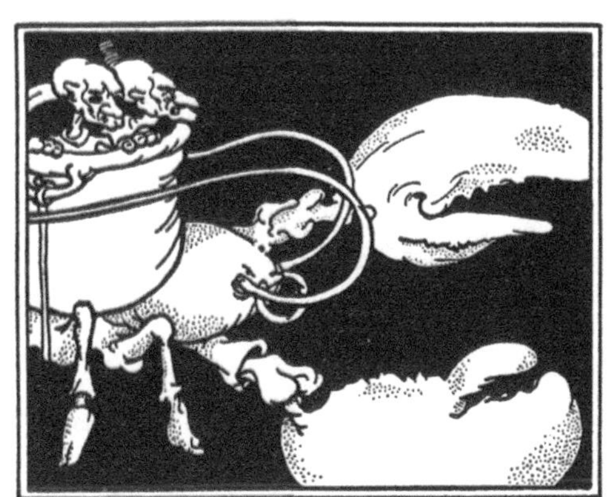

## PART FIRST

# THE SEVENTH OGRE . . .

BLIND MAN once met a deaf man in the woods and they entered into a strange partnership. The blind man was to hear for the deafman and the deafman to see for the blind man.

One day they stopped to watch a snake charmer in the town. The deaf man said

that the snake was very beautiful, but the music not worth listening to; to which the blind man relied:

'On the contrary, my dear partner, the music is refreshing, but the snake is horrible to see.'

Another time, while walking together in the forest, they encountered a huge

lobster with a ring thrust through its nose. On its back it bore a large copper kettle, such as wash women use, filled with brightly colored garments.

Said the deaf man to his blind partner: 'Here is a lobster with a large kettle of clothes on its back. Let us take it with us.'

'Very well,' said the blind man, 'let us take it with us.'

So they proceeded with the lobster and its burden and a little farther on they came to a nest of large black ants.

'Oh!' exclaimed the deaf man, 'a nest of fine black ants, the largest I have ever seen. We shall take a few of them along with us, for we may be able to put them to some good use.'

'Very well,' said the blind man. 'take them along.' So the deaf man took from his pocket a silver snuff box and placed therein four of the larger insects, and they continued their journey.

Before they had travelled many yards a terrific storm arose. Thunder, lightning and rain descended on them with such fury that it seem as though the heavens and the earth were at war.

'Dear me, oh, dear me,' cried the deaf man; 'how terrible is the lightning and rain. Let us seek a place of shelter!'

'Yea, I agree with you concerning the rain,' said the blind man; 'it is most certainly wet. But of the thunder and lightning, the thunder is by far the more terrible. However, let us not argue; it is shelter we need.'

Not far away, on a hill, they found a small wooden door, the entrance to a cave. They opened it and entered, taking the lobster and kettle with them. It did not take the deaf man long to discover that the cave was the home of a wealthy Ogre, as the interior was made as bright as day with the glitter of thousands and thousands of precious stones and pieces of gold and silver. It surrounded them in heaps and in huge jars.

## THE SEVENTH OGRE . . .

'Goodness!' exclaimed the deaf man.

"What is it? asked his partner, because he could not see the treasure.

'Tis a wealth of treasure. There is enough here to make us very rich if we can but carry part of it with us before its owner shall return.' But as he said this, the deaf man saw what made his hair stand on end and his blood run cold. Across the floor came a most hideous monster, long, green, and slimy, while above him soared a huge bat, as large as an ox, and as he flew his wings clattered like dry bones. Then from all sides they came, hundreds of them, from behind the jars and heaps of gold and silver.

The deaf man's teeth chattered as he told the blind man what he saw, and he could not move with fear.

But the blind man could not see and so was not afraid. On the contrary, he became very bold and cried out in his most terrible voice, 'Bally hoo-oo-oo!'

The monsters, never having seen humans before, and thinking misfortune might come from the hands of these odd looking creatures, were really more frightened than the deaf man. And when the blind man shouted at them they scattered for a place to hide. So eager were they to get away that they trampled each other under foot and many were killed in the flight.

'Good work,' said the deaf man, 'I could not have done better myself. Now we must make haste and load the lobster with as much of the treasure as he can carry and get away before the Ogre returns.'

So they began to collect the treasure. The blind man held the sacks while the deaf man filled them. But no sooner had they started to load the lobster than the blind man heard a loud roaring from without.

# . . . THE SEVENTH OGRE

## PART SECOND

## THE SEVENTH OGRE . . .

OH.' exclaimed the blind man, 'I believe that I hear the owner returning. What shall we do?'

'I do not know,' replied the deaf man, beginning to quiver in his boots.

'But wait; perhaps we can frighten him away with the lobster,' suggested the blind man.

LEE BROWN COYE - 1932 -

So they covered the hind quarters of the lobster with the brightly colored clothes and just as the Ogre was about to break in the door, they push the odd looking creature out backwards.

'What's this, what's this!' cried the Ogre, very much surprised at beholding so strange a figure at his door.

'The devil himself!' shouted the blind man.

'Ho,ho!' cried the Ogre, 'you don't expect me to believe that, do you?' For he suspected that some one was after his treasure. But the blind man replied: 'You will believe me after I've bitten off your head' . . . speaking for the lobster.

'If you are the devil himself, let me hear you yell. 'Tis said that the devil yells most terribly.'

Then the deaf man put two of the

large ants in each ear of the lobster. The insects bit the poor animal so that he brought forth a loud, terrible squeal, flapping his bedecked tail as he did so. Then the Ogre, thinking that surely it was the devil himself, turned and fled in great haste.

When the deaf man saw that the Ogre had been frightened away, he took the blind man by the hand and said: "Fine, fine! I could not have done better myself.' Then they set forth, each carrying a large sack of treasure, and with the kettle loaded on the lobster.

But the Ogre, though they had frightened him away, had not gone far and was hiding near-by, that he might see what the devil himself looked like in the daylight. He was watching attentively when out came only a blind man, a deaf

man, and a lobster, all heavily laden with treasure.

This made him very angry and he went immediately to seek his Ogre friends to help him kill the blind man, the deaf man, and the lobster, and regain his treasure. He returned with six other Ogres and when the deaf man saw them coming with their moustaches waving in the stirring breeze, and their huge teeth pointing to the four winds, he became dreadfully frightened.

'They are coming, seven horrible Ogres, to kill us and take the treasure! What shall we do?' he cried.

'Hide the treasure in the bushes,' said the blind man, for as he could not see the Ogres he was not afraid; 'then lead me to a tree and we shall climb into its branches where we will be out of their way.'

Following this advice, the deaf man pushed the lobster into the bushes and placed the rest of the treasure beside it.

THE SEVENTH OGRE . . .

Then he led the blind man to a tall tree, but instead of helping him he scrambled up first and left the poor blind man to climb as best he could.

When the enraged Ogres arrived they held a council to decide what was best to do. Finally the Seventh Ogre suggested that they climb up on each other's shoulders to reach the two unfortunates. So one Ogre stooped down, and the second climbed on his shoulders, and the third on his, and the fourth on his, and the fifth on his, and the sixth on his; and the Seventh Ogre, the owners of the cave, was just climbing up when the deaf man became terribly frightened. Thinking to save himself, he gave his partner a push that sent the poor man sprawling onto the shoulders of the Seventh Ogre. Nor did he realize where he was because he

could not see, and reached out his hand for something to grasp.

Thinking he was on a branch of the tree, he grabbed each of the Ogre's huge leaf-like ears and pinched them very hard in his effort to maintain his balance. The first Ogre could not see what was happening and when the added weight of the blind man came upon him unexpectedly, he lost his balance and fell to the ground, and was followed by the second, third, fourth, fifth, sixth, and seventh Ogres, so that they all lay in a confused heap at the foot of the tree.

Meanwhile the blind man knew not what was occurring and called to his friend, 'Where am I?'

'You're all right!' shouted his deaf partner. 'Hang on and I will be right down to help you!' But he had no intention of forsaking his safe perch. Instead he called: 'Hold on! Hold on!'

The louder he called the harder the blind man pinched the ears of the Seventh Ogre, and the six other Ogres, thinking that they had had enough of helping their friend, after much kicking, extricated themselves and ran away as fast as they could. Then the seventh, thinking that sure enough the devil himself was pinching his ears, shook himself free and ran to his comrades.

As soon as they were out of sight the deaf man very courageously came down from the tree and helped the blind man to his feet, embraced him, and said: 'Well done, brother; I could not have done better myself!'

# PART THIRD

# THE SEVENTH OGRE . . .

HEN they dragged the lobster and the treasure out from the bushes and started once more on their journey. When they were out of the woods and into the light of day the deaf man said: 'We are out in the daylight now and liable to be held up and robbed. I think 'tis best what we divide the treasure, you taking your share, and I mine.'

'An excellent idea,' replied the blind man; 'give me my half, and you take care of your share.'

But the cunning deaf man had no intention of giving the blind man half of the treasure, so he put a small amount of it in two sacks and gave the blind man one. 'Here, partner, is your share,' he said.

The blind man put down his hand to pick up his sack, and when he felt so small a bundle he cried: 'You have cheated me. You have kept most of the treasure for yourself and have given me only a small part of it!'

'Oh, oh, how can you think so ill of me, brother,' said the deaf man; 'but if you do not believe me, feel my sack of treasure. It is no larger than your own.'

The blind man put out his hands to feel how much the deaf man had kept, and when he found only as much as he himself had, became very angry and cried: 'You intend to rob me because I am blind, but I am not stupid. I had all that I could bear, and you had likewise, and out friend the lobster was laden with as much, yet you would make me believe that the treasure has shrunk.'

And so they continued arguing, bickering, and growling until the blind man became so enraged that he gave the deaf man a terrific box on the ear. The blow was so violent that the deaf man was made to hear. The deaf man was so incensed, however, that he gave his partner so tremendous a blow in the face that it opened the blind man's eyes.

. . . THE SEVENTH OGRE

So the blind man could see as well as hear, and the deaf man could hear as well as see. They were both so astonished that they shook hands and agreed to become friends once more. The deaf man then dragged the remainder of the treasure from its hiding place and they once more set out in high spirits.

As they were walking the ex-blind man said: 'It would be truly fine if we found a little house in which to live together.'

'Excellent, brother,' said the ex-deaf man; 'perhaps we may be able to buy such a place with our wealth.' And they had not travelled far when they came upon a small house in a clump of trees.

'Here is what we want,' they both exclaimed; 'perhaps the own might agree to see to us. Let us inquire.' So they went to the door and knocked, but instead of a plumb farmer's wife, as they had expected, there appeared a most horrible looking witch.

'Oh!' from the deaf man, and 'Oh, oh!' from the blind man, and they turned to flee.

'O-o-o-o-o-o!' howled the witch; 'what would you have here?'

But the two were too frightened to answer, and as they ran the silver snuff box fell from the pocket of the deaf man and the huge ants began crawling towards the witch.

'Murder!' she screeched; 'ants; the only thing I fear' 'tis the curse of the Devil!' And with this she ran screaming into the forest, and if she hasn't stopped, she's running yet.

When she had passed from sight the two partners entered the house, but not

before they had tied the ants to the door to assure themselves safety from the witch, should she return.

Inside they found their dream of an

ideal home, containing everything that would be of need to them. And there they lived in peace and happiness for the rest of their days. . . The End

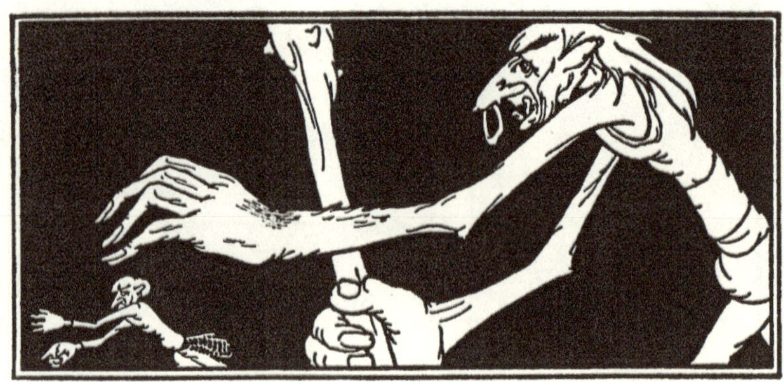

*The original 1932 first edition of* The Seventh Ogre *consisted of three hundred fifty copies, printed for* Lee Brown Coye & Leo Kaplan *by* The Printing House of Leo Hart, *Rochester, New York. This facsimile edition from* Nonstop Press, *New York City, is limited to three hundred copies in hardcover.*

## Afterword
by Luis Ortiz

Lee Brown Coye was born on July 24, 1907, in a house on Sabine Street in Syracuse, New York. Before he was a year old, his parents moved to Tully, New York, a small town eighteen miles south of Syracuse. Growing up Lee was considered a "holy terror," although his mischief chiefly ran to Tom Sawyerish tricks and retorts. By age thirteen Lee was already training himself to be an artist — he had borrowed ***Suggestions for a Course of Instruction in Color*** and ***Free Hand Perspective and Drawing*** from the school library, and both books were long overdue.

At the age of twenty-one, already married to a girl he met on a high school blind-date, Coye moved to Leonia, New Jersey against his father's wishes. For a short time he was part of the art colony there, and took lessons from the woodcut master illustrator Howard McCormick. Up until the stock market debacle in October 1929, Coye had an idea of becoming a cartoonist or children's book illustrator. After the crash he was without job prospects or money, and was forced to return home to upstate New York. In 1930 Lee made his first appearance in a pulp magazine, the July issue of ***Golden Book***.

In 1932 Coye was living in Cortland, NY. He was twenty-five years old and through a mutual friend had been introduced to twenty-year-old Leo Kaplan, a recent graduate from the College of Art & Design at Rochester Institute of Technology. They found they had much in common and together set up the Studio of Coye & Kaplan over a ladies clothing store on Main Street. The studio was little more than an unheated room with two drawing tables. Leo would do catalog illustrations of fishing tackle, corsets, and hardware while Lee worked in his spared time, in some cases all night, on his woodcuts and ink drawings. Coye made his living from sign painting, and he painted a lot of display cards for stores just to get by. Coye remarked about this period: "[...] if I had a week where I made $5 it was a big week. I had a small family. Of course I'm not complaining. I was in the same spot as everyone else."

Coye was a big reader, devouring whatever came his way and had somewhere read the East Indian tale he used as the underpinnings for his first illustrated book. Over the course of a few weeks he created all of the scratchboard illustrations for *The Seventh Ogre.*

Kaplan suggested they publish a limited edition children's book, selling the book themselves and sharing in any profits. Kaplan was already familiar with the printing house of Leo Hart from his school days in Rochester, and arranged to have the book printed there. The firm of Leo Hart was essentially a job printing house, but they also produced small editions of books that sold to collectors.

*The Seventh Ogre* would be Lee's first substantial, unified illustrative work. Kaplan designed the book and typography; Lee supplied the illustrations and adaptation. Coye was also the "corporate" treasurer and when the printer's bill came due he had spent the money on food and clothing for his family. The printer threatened a lawsuit. Kaplan attempted to get the printing plates of the book and take them to a cheaper printer. The plan was to use the money from sales of a second edition to pay Leo Hart, hopefully with enough left to pay the second printer. Horace Hart, president of Leo Hart Printing Company, turned down this scheme. A lawyer friend came to their rescue when he examined the contract and declared it non-binding, since Kaplan had signed it as a minor.

Through most of the 1930s Coye was forced to labor as a malcontented advertising agency art director working on small town accounts appearing in places like the trade magazine ***The Milk Dealer***. In 1934 under the aegis of PWAP, the first federal public works for artists program, he designed and painted (from a 20-foot ladder) a large historical mural in Cazenovia, New York. The mural exhibited the strong influence of Thomas Hart Benton, and was later destroyed when the style of the work was deemed too primal for its intended audience of middle-schoolchildren.

He seemed all set to make a career breakthrough when the Whitney Museum accepted some of his watercolors for its annual exhibitions in 1939 (his work appeared alongside Reginald Marsh, Edward Hopper, and Peggy Bacon) and the New York's Metropolitan Museum of Art brought one of his paintings from the exhibit for its permanent collection. However, with the arrival of abstractionists fleeing war-torn Europe, the fine art world quickly moved in a different direction.

While Coye dabbled in abstract paintings, and worked as a medical artist and cartoonist, he always considered himself primary an illustrator. Much of his art during this period were based on books, including ***Treasure Island*** and stories by Washington Irving. Many of these illustrations were done on scratchboard.

In 1944 Coye stumbled into illustrating a book of horror stories published by Farrar & Rinehart and edited by August Derleth. Coye, who was a fan of ghost tales and fascinated by folk superstitions, fell under the spell of the stories in ***Sleep No More*** and created twenty-five illustrations, dust-jacket art, and a number of drawings that did not make it into the book because the publisher thought them too gruesome — including one piece showing a pair of audaciously detailed hanged men. While working on the drawings he told an interviewer for a Syracuse newspaper, "I love horrific pictures." Two more horror collections from Derleth would follow in 1946 and 1947. For these books Coye designed dozens of diabolic illustrations that veered from childish whimsy to disturbing modernistic freakishness and established him as a horror specialist.

Coye was creating horror art while studying medical anatomy and his studio was a gothic chamber filled with skeletons, dead animals, live rats, and human body parts from a medical college. While reading stories for ***Sleep No More*** in the summer of 1944, Coye had visited the Rockefeller Center offices of the pulp magazine ***Weird Tales*** and found himself making some drawings for quick money.

He quickly became a popular and prolific ***Weird Tales***

artist, appearing in many issues from 1945 to 1952 — sometimes four and five times in a single issue, and created a running full page illustration titled "Weirdisms". His illustrations in ***Weird Tales*** managed to mix the macabre with humor. Any fame he has today comes from his uniquely strange and vivid artwork in ***Weird Tales***.

In 1962 Coye returned to horror illustration, after a ten-year hiatus, when he contacted Arkham House, Derleth's publishing concern (specializing in the writings of H.P. Lovecraft), with the hope of getting dust-jacket art assignments.

Coye's second association with Derleth culminated in the illustrated masterpiece: Lovecraft's ***3 Tales of Horror (1967)***. Executed over the span of four years, his drawings for the book seem to give off a visceral menace. After Derleth's death in 1971, Coye illustrated books published by Carcosa, a small press run in the Arkham House mode by Karl Edward Wagner, Jim Groce and David Drake.

Coye died in 1981, after a stroke that had partially paralyzed him and kept him in nursing homes and hospitals for the last four years of his life. He left behind a body of work that jibed with much of the morbidity of the twentieth-century.

- LEE BROWN COYE 1932

# OTHER BOOKS FROM NONSTOP PRESS

**Lord of Darkness** by Robert Silverberg
Trade paper $17.95 (ISBN: 978-1-933065-43-4; *ebook available*)

"... gripping and compulsively readable." — George R.R. Martin

SET in the 17th century and based on a true-life historical figure, this novel is a tale of exotic lands, romance, and hair-raising adventures. Andrew Battell is a buccaneer on a British ship when he is taken prisoner by Portuguese pirates. Injured and ailing, Andrew is brought to the west coast of Africa where his only solace is Dona Teresa, a young woman who nurses him back to health. Andrew's sole hope to return home is to first serve his Portuguese masters, but it is a hope that dwindles as he is pulled further and further into the interior of the continent, into the land of the Jaqqa — the region's most fierce and feared cannibal tribe — overseen by the powerful Lord of Darkness. This story demonstrates the timelessness of any great adventure and the determination to persevere at any cost.

**The Very Best of Barry N. Malzberg** Introduction by Joe Wrzos

Trade paper $14.95 (ISBN: 978-1-933065-41-0; *ebook available*)

FOR NEARLY half a century Barry N. Malzberg has been stretching the boundaries of science fiction and fantasy. Each of the 37 stories in this compilation offers Malzberg's trademark vision of a future that is equal parts cautionary tale and social commentary. These hand-picked selections exhibit his versatile imagination and the dark humor so characteristic of his work.

**Meeting the Dog Girls,** stories by Gay Partington Terry
Trade paper $14.95 (ISBN 978-1933065-20-5; *ebook available*)

"... nonpareil fantastika that will stay with you for a long time."
— *Asimov's Science Fiction Magazine*

A THIEF, languishing in prison for stealing moments, escapes and becomes a chronometric fugitive. Women wait in a long, endless line, night and day, without knowing what is at the beginning of the line. An otherworldly marble called the Ustek Cloudy passes through the hands of Ambrose Bierce, Amelia Earhart, and D. B. Cooper just before they each disappear off the face of the earth. Whether they are called fantasy, magical realism, science fiction, or brilliant parodies, the stories in this collection—the first from Gay Terry—blend the real and the fantastic in an imaginative and mischievous way. Written in the tradition of Ray Bradbury, Angela Carter, and Neil Gaiman, these contemporary fables present remarkable characters trapped in unusual situations.

**The Collected Stories of Carol Emshwiller Vol. 1 & 2**

Hardcover

"... offers not only hours of pleasure through its dozens of wonderful, magical stories, but also the rare joy of seeing a master's work develop over decades."
— *Strange Horizons*

A MASSIVE NEW COLLECTION of 88 stories. Carol Emshwiller's fiction cuts a straight path through the landscape of American literary genres: mystery, speculative fiction, magic realism, western, slipstream, fantasy and of course science fiction. Arranged chronologically, this landmark collection, the first of two volumes, allows the reader to see Emshwiller's development as a writer and easily recognize her as a major voice in the literary landscape.

**The Science Fiction Fanzine Reader: Focal Points, 1930-1960**
Edited by Luis Ortiz    Hardcover and Trade paper

THE FIRST MAINSTREAM BOOK to go into the background of fanzine culture and shed light on how science fiction fandom has shaped popular culture. Editor Luis Ortiz with his sweeping knowledge and passion for the genre has mined thousands of fanzines to collect more than 50 essays by participants in the genesis of American science fiction. The book is a paean to the young writers and artists that would grow up to define the field. People like Ray Bradbury, Harlan Ellison, Donald A. Wollheim, Marion Zimmer Bradley, Robert Silverberg, and many more.

**Steampunk Prime: A Vintage Steampunk Reader**
Edited by Mike Ashley, with a foreword by Paul di Filippo, illustrated by Luis Ortiz.

Trade paper $15.95 (ISBN 978-1933065182; *ebook available*)

"These tales have the pulpy goodness steampunk fans adore...."
— *Publishers Weekly*

"Within this collection, readers will find romance, mystery, adventure, and, of course, the iconic steampunk airship." — *School Library Journal*

**Science Fiction: The 101 Best Novels —1985-2010**
by Damien Broderick and Paul Di Filippo.

Trade paper $14.99 (ISBN: 978-1-933065-39-7; *ebook available*)

"If you want to know the essential science-fiction books to read that were published in the last 25 years, this is your go-to guide." — *Kirkus*

INSPIRED by David Pringle's landmark volume, SCIENCE FICTION: THE 100 BEST NOVELS, which appeared in 1985, this volume will supplement the earlier selection with the authors' choice of the best SF novels issued in English during the past quarter-century. David Pringle provides a foreword.

*Nonstop Library of American Artists*

**Vol. 1: Arts Unknown: The Life & Art of Lee Brown Coye** by Luis Ortiz; $39.95 Hardcover (ISBN: 978-1-933065-04-4) *Fully illustrated, color.*

"A must for lovers of the weird and fantastic." — *Publishers Weekly*

"A smashingly beautiful book … reading this fine biography is like riding a train through the history of three-quarters of the 20th century, and seeing Coye's monsters through every window." —*Asimov's Science Fiction Magazine*

**Vol. 2: Emshwiller: Infinity x Two**
**The Art & Life of Ed & Carol Emshwiller** by Luis Ortiz; $39.95 Hardcover (ISBN: 978-1-933065-08-3) *Fully illustrated, color*

"… fascinating …. a must have for anyone interested in SF art, writing, and history."– *LOCUS*

*A 2008 Hugo Award nominee and Locus Award finalist.*

**Vol. 3: Outermost: The Art + Life of Jack Gaughan** by Luis Ortiz; $39.95 hardcover (ISBN: 978-1-933065-16-8) *Fully illustrated, color*

FANTASTIC IMAGERY, explosive color, and occasionally creepy creations merge together in this elaborate collection of the work of genius artist, Jack Gaughan. Extremely prolific and popular from the 1960s through the 1980s, Gaughan is showcased in this chronicle that is the first to detail the art and life of this master of the science fiction and fantasy genre. Overflowing with samples of work from the artist's personal archives and exploring examples of his working method, this definitive guide provides an inside look into this four time Hugo Award winner.

. . . .

**Cult Magazines: From A to Z, A Compendium of Culturally Obsessive & Curiously Expressive Publications**
Edited by Earl Kemp & Luis Ortiz

"Contains a wealth of arcane information about many of the oddball magazines that once graced newsstands." — *New York Times Book Review*

Oversized trade paper, $34.95 (ISBN: 978-1-933065-14-4)

Featuring full-color reproductions of hundreds of distinctive cult magazine cover images, this reference's backgrounds, histories, and essays offer a complete picture of a bygone era. ***Fully illustrated in color.***

**www.nonstoppress.com**

www.ingramcontent.com/pod-product-compliance
Lightning Source LLC
Chambersburg PA
CBHW030612310726
48979CB00003B/676

* 9 7 8 1 9 3 3 0 6 5 6 5 6 *